MW01379551

TOP 10
STARS OF THE NCAA MEN'S BASKETBALL TOURNAMENT

Ron Knapp

SPORTS TOP 10

Enslow Publishers, Inc.

40 Industrial Road	PO Box 38
Box 398	Aldershot
Berkeley Heights, NJ 07922	Hants GU12 6BP
USA	UK

http://www.enslow.com

For Marcus Teubert, champion golfer

Library of Congress Cataloging-in-Publication Data

Knapp, Ron.
  Top 10 stars of the NCAA men's basketball tournament / Ron Knapp.
    p. cm. — (Sports top 10)
  Includes bibliographical references and index.
  ISBN 0-7660-1498-3
    1. Basketball players—United States—Biography—Juvenile literature.
  2. National Collegiate Athletic Association—Biography—Juvenile literature.
  [1. Basketball players.] I. Title: Top ten stars of the NCAA men's basketball tournament. II. Title. III. Series.
  GV884.A1 K639   2001
  796.323'092'273—dc21

                                                          00-12220

Printed in the United States of America

10 9 8 7 6 5 4 3 2 1

To Our Readers: We have done our best to make sure all Internet addresses in this book were active and appropriate when we went to press. However, the author and the publisher have no control over and assume no liability for the material available on those Internet sites or on other Web sites they may link to. Any comments or suggestions can be sent by e-mail to comments@enslow.com or to the address on the back cover.

Illustration Credits: AP/Wide World Photos, pp. 6, 9, 21, 29, 35, 37, 38, 41, 42, 45; ASUCLA Photo Dept., pp. 10, 13, 14, 17; Bob Kalmbach, pp. 30; © Mitchell Layton/Newsport, pp. 19, 23, 25, 33; University of North Carolina, pp. 27.

Cover Illustration: AP/Wide World Photos.

Cover Description: Christian Laettner.

CONTENTS

INTRODUCTION	4
BILL BRADLEY	6
KAREEM ABDUL-JABBAR	10
BILL WALTON	14
MAGIC JOHNSON	18
ISIAH THOMAS	22
JAMES WORTHY	26
GLEN RICE	30
CHRISTIAN LAETTNER	34
MILES SIMON	38
RICHARD HAMILTON	42
CHAPTER NOTES	46
INDEX	48

Introduction

The Biggest Tournament in College Sports got its start as a copycat. Back in 1938, the National Collegiate Athletic Association (NCAA) was a quiet group that worked to make sure all colleges played by the same rules.

That was the year sportswriters organized the first National Invitational Tournament (NIT) at Madison Square Garden in New York City. Six teams were invited after the regular season ended. The event was a success, and NCAA officials decided to have a tournament of their own. The first one, with eight teams, ended when Oregon beat Ohio State for the 1939 title, 46–33.

For the next decade, American colleges had two important postseason basketball tournaments. The NCAA tourney usually featured the winners of the big conferences across the nation, while the NIT invited the top independent teams. Sometimes the winners of the two tournaments met in a national championship game.

But in the 1950s, the NCAA tournament gradually emerged as the most important postseason action. The only teams who went to the NIT were the ones who had not qualified for the NCAA event.

Over the years, the NCAA began expanding the field. By 1975, thirty-two teams qualified. Ten years later the field had doubled to sixty-four. There was room, finally, for good teams that had not won their conferences.

Today millions of American sports fans study the brackets and follow their favorite teams. Nothing else seems to matter on that first Monday night in April when the two survivors meet in the NCAA Final. After that game, there is no doubt about which team is the national champion.

Each athlete in this book was honored as the Most Outstanding Player (MOP) of the Final Four. Maybe you do not agree with all of our choices. Where's Wilt Chamberlain? Or Jerry Lucas and Bill Russell? Or even Alex Groza?

In this book there is only room for ten. We hope you will agree that our ten choices have helped make the NCAA Tournament the spectacular event it has become.

FINAL FOUR STATISTICS

Player	YR	G	FG%	FT%	REB	AST	STL	RPG	PPG
BILL BRADLEY	1965	2	.630	.950	24	*	*	12.0	43.5
KAREEM ABDUL-JABBAR	1967–69	6	.641	.610	113	*	*	18.8	25.7
BILL WALTON	1972–73	4	.762	.679	71	*	*	17.8	28.8
MAGIC JOHNSON	1979	2	.680	.864	17	3	2	8.5	26.5
ISIAH THOMAS	1981	2	.560	.818	4	9	4	2.0	18.5
JAMES WORTHY	1982	2	.741	.286	8	9	4	4.0	21.0
GLEN RICE	1989	2	.490	1.000	16	1	3	8.0	29.5
CHRISTIAN LAETTNER	1991	2	.545	.913	17	2	2	8.5	23.0
MILES SIMON	1997	2	.459	.773	8	6	1	4.0	27.0
RICHARD HAMILTON	1999	2	.513	.727	12	4	2	6.0	25.5

All stats include only Final Four games from the years in which the player won the Most Outstanding Player award.

YR=YEARS IN FINAL FOUR   **FT%**=FREE THROW PERCENTAGE   **STL**=STEALS
G=GAMES   **REB**=REBOUNDS   **RPG**=REBOUNDS PER GAME
FG%=FIELD GOAL PERCENTAGE   **AST**=ASSISTS   **PPG**= POINTS PER GAME

* Statistics are incomplete for some players in some categories.

BILL BRADLEY

Bill Bradley is shown here in a photo from 1964. Bradley excelled at Princeton University as both a student and an athlete.

BILL BRADLEY

BILL BRADLEY IS THE ONLY ATHLETE in this book who has not played for an NCAA champion. That, however, is not the only fact that makes him unique.

Unlike many athletes, Bradley had no money problems when he was growing up. His family was wealthy. Each winter when it got cold in Crystal City, Missouri, the Bradleys moved to Florida for a few months.

Differing from some gifted athletes, Bradley always worked hard to improve his skills. When he was fourteen, his height was already six feet three inches—and he was already spending four hours a day practicing his shooting.

Unlike most good basketball players, at first Bradley could not jump very high. To strengthen his jumping muscles, he attached weights to his shoes.

Following a separate path than most high school athletes, Bradley did not choose the college with the best basketball program. Instead, he picked Princeton University because of its reputation as a tough school with excellent academics.

In his first year on the Princeton varsity team, he helped take the team to the 1963 NCAA tournament. Even though the Tigers lost to St. Joseph's, 82–81, Bradley scored 40 points.

When he was a junior, he averaged 32.2 points per game. That season, Princeton was knocked out of the post-season tournament in the second round.

In 1964, Bradley was the youngest member of the gold-medal-winning U.S. Olympic basketball team in Tokyo, Japan.

During the following season he broke the hearts of Penn

State fans in the opening round of the 1965 NCAA Tournament. Late in the game the Nittany Lions went ahead four times, and each time Bradley scored to tie it up again. Finally, Princeton won, 60–58. After defeating North Carolina State and Providence, Bradley's team was the surprise squad in the Final Four. Fans started pulling for the underdog Ivy League school. Bradley's high-scoring heroics made him a favorite.

Cazzie Russell and the Michigan Wolverines were heavily favored to whip Princeton in the semifinal game. But Bradley and his teammates surprised everybody by going twelve minutes without missing a shot. The Tigers led, 34–29, but then foul trouble sent Bradley to the bench. The Wolverines rallied and won the game, 93–76.

In the consolation game, Bradley turned in his final performance as a college athlete. It was quite a show. Butch van Breda Kolff, the Tigers coach, told him to take all the shots he could. Most of them went in. When he left the floor with 58 points, the fans stood for the longest ovation in the tournament's history.

"The 1965 Final Four holds very special memories for me," Bradley said. "It was a culmination of all of my work and the team's work during my years at Princeton."[1]

After studying in England as a Rhodes Scholar, he finally joined the NBA in 1967. He helped the New York Knicks take championships in 1970 and 1973.

Unlike many other retired players, Bradley did not try for a career as a coach or a broadcaster. Instead, he went into politics. He served three terms as a U.S. senator from New Jersey. Bill Bradley even made a serious run for the U.S. presidency in 2000. After months of campaigning, he lost the Democratic nomination to Vice President Al Gore. Gore eventually lost the presidential election to George W. Bush.

Born: July 28, 1943, Crystal City, Missouri.

High School: Bismarck High School, Crystal City, Missouri.

College: Princeton University.

Pro: New York Knicks, 1967–1977.

Records: Set NCAA Tournament Final Four single-game record for points scored (58).

Honors: Olympic Gold Medalist, 1964; three-time All-American Collegian; College Player of the Year, 1965; NCAA Tournament MVP, 1965; Sullivan Award, 1965; Rhodes Scholar.

Bill Bradley takes a pass from Princeton teammate William Kock in a game from 1965.

Internet Address

http://www.hoophall.com/halloffamers/Bradley.htm

UCLA center Lew Alcindor, later known as Kareem Abdul-Jabbar, skies high above the rim.

KAREEM ABDUL-JABBAR

WHEN KAREEM ABDUL-JABBAR WAS a thirteen-year-old growing up in New York City, his name was still Lew Alcindor. In an eighth-grade game, he took "a real nice pass on the fast break. The ball came into my hands and I was able to jam it. . . . A moment of elation on the court I have never forgotten."[1]

By the time he was a seven-foot-tall high school senior, Alcindor was the most heavily recruited star in the nation. He decided to play for John Wooden at the University of California at Los Angeles (UCLA).

Wooden's Bruins were the defending NCAA champions. But in a 1965 practice game, they were whipped by Alcindor and the UCLA freshmen, 75–60. Luckily for the other teams, freshmen at that time were ineligible to play college varsity ball.

In his first varsity game, Alcindor hit 56 points. He led UCLA to thirty straight victories. In the NCAA Quarterfinals, the Bruins ran into Elvin "Big E" Hayes and the Houston Cougars. The Cougars had a 19–18 edge, but then the Bruins got eleven straight points to put the game out of reach. In the final, UCLA led Dayton, 76–47, with five minutes to go. The game was out of reach, so Wooden pulled his starters. UCLA finally won, 79–64.

The college rules committee tried to tame the Bruins by adopting the "Alcindor Rule." Dunks were banned. Alcindor just switched to a hook shot. When a seven-foot two-inch athlete lets loose a hook shot, it is almost impossible to stop. Alcindor's fans called it the "sky hook."

UCLA was again undefeated midway through the 1967–68 season. Then came the "Game of the Decade." In front of fifty thousand screaming fans at the Astrodome, the Bruins once again met Big E and the Houston Cougars.

Hayes was fantastic. He scored 29 points in the first half, then helped fight off UCLA in the closing minutes. After the game, Big E said that Alcindor was overrated.

Alcindor kept his mouth shut. He did not make a big deal out of the fact that he had been hospitalized days before with a scratched cornea. Instead, he just remembered everything Hayes said and taped a picture of the Cougar star to his locker door.

Big E and Big Lew met again in the 1968 NCAA Quarterfinals. This time Hayes had only 10 points. Every Bruin starter scored at least 14. UCLA won, 101–69.

In the Final, Alcindor swatted away North Carolina shots like they were pesky mosquitoes. The Tar Heels fell, 78–55.

Late in the 1968–69 season, the University of Southern California (USC) beat UCLA, 46–44, with a last-second shot. It was only the second game Alcindor's Bruins team ever lost. And the last. In the 1969 title game, UCLA surged to a 26–10 lead, then buried Purdue, 92–72.

The Age of Alcindor was finally over, but what a three-year trip it had been. Eighty-eight victories in ninety games. Three national championships. Three NCAA tournament MOP trophies, and a three-time All-American.

Only one thing changed when Lew Alcindor moved to the pros—his name. After reading *The Autobiography of Malcolm X*, he converted to Islam and changed his name to Kareem Abdul-Jabbar, which means "Noble and Generous Servant of the All-Powerful Allah."

Abdul-Jabbar was the NBA Rookie of the Year in 1970. Six times he was the league MVP. His teams won six NBA titles.

KAREEM ABDUL-JABBAR

BORN: April 16, 1947, New York, New York.

HIGH SCHOOL: Power Memorial, New York, New York.

COLLEGE: University of California at Los Angeles (UCLA).

PRO: Milwaukee Bucks, 1969–1975; Los Angeles Lakers, 1975–1989.

RECORDS: Holds NBA career records for most minutes played (57,446), most points (38,387), and most field goals (15,837).

HONORS: College Player of the Year, 1967, 1969; NCAA Tournament MVP, 1967, 1968, 1969; NBA Rookie of the Year, 1970; NBA MVP 1971, 1972, 1974, 1976, 1977, 1980; elected to Basketball Hall of Fame, 1995; selected as one of the 50 Greatest Players in NBA History, 1996.

Jabbar led UCLA to three consecutive NCAA championships. In the process he became the only player to win three Most Outstanding Player awards.

Internet Address

http://www.hoophall.com/halloffamers/Abdul-Jabbar.htm

BILL WALTON

Bill Walton jumps above the competition to win the tip-off for his team.

BILL WALTON

THE TALL, SKINNY REDHEAD DID NOT want to come out of the bathroom.

"You're nervous, aren't you?" asked his coach, Rocky Graciano.

"I'm real nervous," admitted twelve-year-old Bill Walton. Their seventh grade team at Blessed Sacrament Elementary School was playing for the league championship.

"Bill, you've got to learn to love these moments because this is what sports is all about, playing for the championship. You're going to play in a lot of these championship games before you're through, and you have to look forward to each one as if it's the greatest opportunity and the greatest moment in your life."[1] Bill Walton finally came out of the bathroom—and he led his team to the league title.

After leading Helix High School to a 35–0 record as a senior, Walton was the most heavily recruited high school basketball star in the country. He chose to attend nearby UCLA, where John Wooden had just coached his team to a fifth straight NCAA title.

In the 1971–72 season, when Walton joined the Bruins varsity, he stood six feet eleven inches tall. He averaged 21.1 points and 15 rebounds a game that year. The team went undefeated for the regular season, beating their opponents by an average margin of 30.3 points a game.

They slashed their way through the early rounds of the 1972 NCAA Championships, setting up a title game with the Florida State Seminoles. At first, it looked like the Bruins might be in trouble. Walton was double-teamed by a pair of Seminoles who were both as tall as he was. When he had trouble getting the ball, UCLA had trouble scoring. Early in the game, Florida State led by seven points.

Walton eventually began slipping past the other big men, the points went in, and Florida State's margin disappeared. When it was over, UCLA had an 81–76 victory and another national championship. Walton had 24 points and MOP honors.

In the 1972–73 season the Bruins were again undefeated heading into the tournament final. They would face the Memphis State Tigers. "They were not particularly tall, so we tried to go to the hoop with the ball," Walton later said.[2] But Memphis State had a plan. When Walton closed in on the basket with the ball, three defenders surrounded him. He got three quick fouls and had to do a lot of sitting.

When he finally got back into the game, Walton had a plan of his own. "What do you say you throw it up high, and I'll go over the top for a layup?" he told his teammates.[3] Because of his long arms, the alley-oop pass worked again and again. Walton took 22 shots and missed only one. It was one of the greatest pressure performances in sports history. UCLA won, 87–66.

The 1973–74 season looked as if it would be more of the same. The Bruins had 88 wins in a row when they ran into Notre Dame. With less than four minutes left, the streak looked safe. UCLA led by eleven points, but Notre Dame came back to pull off a stunning upset.

There was an even bigger shock in the postseason: North Carolina State knocked UCLA out of the NCAA tournament in the Semifinals.

Injuries shortened Walton's professional career in the NBA, but he was on two more championship teams. With the big redhead leading the way, the Portland Trailblazers won in 1977. Finally, he came off the bench to help Larry Bird and the Boston Celtics take the 1986 title.

BILL WALTON

BORN: November 5, 1952, La Mesa, California.

HIGH SCHOOL: Helix High School, La Mesa, California.

COLLEGE: UCLA.

PRO: Portland Trailblazers, 1974–1979; San Diego Clippers, 1979–1984; Los Angeles Clippers, 1984–1985; Boston Celtics, 1985–1987.

RECORDS: NCAA Tournament career record for field-goal percentage, 68.6 percent.

HONORS: College Player of the Year, 1972–1974; NCAA Tournament MVP, 1972, 1973; NBA Playoff MVP, 1977; NBA MVP, 1978; elected to Basketball Hall of Fame, 1993; selected as one of the 50 Greatest Players in NBA History, 1996.

Bill Walton won the Naismith Award as college basketball's premier player three times at UCLA.

Internet Address

http://www.nba.com/history/walton_bio.html

Magic Johnson

In the 1980s, the NBA Was in Trouble. Attendance was down. Television networks were cutting back the games they broadcast. Fans seemed to be losing interest in professional basketball.

Then came Larry Bird and Earvin Johnson. Bird, a six-foot nine-inch forward with long, curly blond hair, led the Boston Celtics to three NBA titles in the 1980s. Johnson and the Los Angeles Lakers won five. Between them, they shared five Finals MVP awards and six regular-season MVPs. Their rivalry brought the fans back to the NBA.

Bird and Johnson first met in the 1979 NCAA Final. By then, Johnson was already one of the most popular athletes in the country. Johnson was big—six feet eight inches and two hundred pounds—but he played point guard, not center. A big man with great ball-handling skills was very tough to stop. Johnson was so good he earned the nickname Magic.

In the 1978–79 season, Johnson's sophomore year at Michigan State University, his passing, shooting, teamwork, and leadership helped carry the Spartans to the NCAA Final. There they faced Larry the Legend and Indiana State University. Even when he had been double- and triple-teamed, Bird and the Sycamores managed to beat all their opponents. Going into the Final, they were 32–0.

Spartans head coach Jud Heathcote told his men to smother Bird every time he got the ball. The plan worked. Bird was stopped. "I could see it in his eyes that he was frustrated," said Magic's teammate Terry Donnelly. "He'd go

Magic Johnson beats his man to the basket for two easy points.

up in the air, pump two or three times looking for the pass, then he'd wind up shooting on the way down."[1]

Midway through the second half, the Spartans had fought their way to a 16-point lead . . . but the game was not over yet. They were in foul trouble: Greg Kelser had 4, Johnson and Ron Charles 3 apiece. With starters on the bench, Heathcote was afraid Bird might take over the game.

The Spartans tried to hold the ball and stall. But a few passes were flubbed, and they started getting sloppy on defense. The Sycamores began nibbling away at the lead. "We were worried," Donnelly admitted.[2]

With just over five minutes left, Johnson crashed the hoop with a thunderous slam dunk. He soon added a pair of free throws and the Spartans were up, 61–50.

The tight Michigan State defense resulted in a lot of fouls, but the Sycamores did not have much luck at the free-throw line. They made only ten of twenty-two tries. Bird was just as cold from the floor. He shot twenty-one times, but made just seven baskets. Despite his reputation as a great passer, he picked up only two assists.

Johnson's 24 points, 7 rebounds, and 5 assists paced a 75–64 Michigan State victory. "The Magic Man directed the show and we got good basketball out of the rest of the team," said Heathcote.[3]

Johnson flashed his famous smile and told reporters, "When the time comes, I'm the Magic Man."[4]

A few weeks later, with the NCAA title under his belt, Johnson left college basketball. That fall he joined another college champion, Kareem Abdul-Jabbar, with the Los Angeles Lakers.

After twelve incredible seasons as a pro, Magic retired after contracting HIV. Since his retirement, he has remained in the public eye as a successful businessman, television personality, and spokesman for HIV/AIDS prevention.

Magic Johnson

Born: August 14, 1959, Lansing, Michigan.

High School: Everett High School, Lansing, Michigan.

College: Michigan State University.

Pro: Los Angeles Lakers, 1979–1991, 1996.

Records: Holds NBA career playoff records for assists (2,346) and steals (358).

Honors: NCAA Tournament MVP, 1979; NBA MVP, 1987, 1989, 1990; NBA Playoff MVP, 1980, 1982, 1987; Olympic gold medalist, 1992; selected as one of the 50 Greatest Players in NBA History, 1996.

Magic Johnson slam dunks the ball in the NCAA championship game on March 27, 1979.

Internet Address

http://espn.go.com/classic/biography/s/johnson_magic.html

ISIAH THOMAS

THE HOOSIERS' BIG-TIME PLAYER was six-foot one-inch Isiah Thomas, a flashy guard who had never seemed to get along with Coach Bobby Knight. When the coach visited the Thomas home, he almost got into a fight with Isiah's brother. When Thomas played in the 1979 Pan American Games, Knight told him not to bother coming to Indiana, but Isiah came anyway. Many times he irritated his coach by not following directions on the court or by causing turnovers.

For example, in a game against the North Carolina Tar Heels, Thomas threw away two balls; Knight benched him. The Hoosiers lost by nine points.

For the 1981 NCAA crown, Indiana would be facing the same North Carolina team. By then Knight seemed to be happy with his star. He had made Thomas a co-captain. After a pretty rough season, did he think his team had a chance? "We lost nine games," Knight said, "but those games prepared us for this. I've never seen a group of kids stay with a goal or work harder."[1]

The Tar Heels took control of the game early, jumping to a 16–8 lead. The Hoosiers did not get their first lead until Randy Wittman's twenty-foot jumper ended the first half and put Indiana ahead, 27–26.

As the second half began, North Carolina was moving the ball slowly down the court. Thomas was in no mood for slow-paced action. He stripped the ball from Jimmy Black and took off in the opposite direction. Easy layup!

The Tar Heels tried again. This time Isiah intercepted a pass. Another layup!

ISIAH THOMAS

Isiah Thomas is shown here during his years with the Detroit Pistons. Thomas went pro after leading Indiana to the 1981 NCAA Championship.

"Those two Thomas baskets were the turning point," said Dean Smith, the North Carolina coach. "He really broke it open."[2]

The Tar Heels were in trouble. Indiana outscored them 18–8 during the first ten minutes of the second half. Then the Hoosiers shifted strategy. Slow things down, Knight told them. Play tight defense. Wait for a good shot. Make North Carolina work hard for any points.

The strategy worked. Even though Indiana hit only two baskets in the last twelve minutes, the lead held. The Tar Heels were forced to play aggressive defense to try to take the ball away. Again and again they were whistled for fouls. Again and again the Hoosiers made the free throws.

Meanwhile the Indiana defense was solid. Landon Turner had shut down Sam Perkins, North Carolina's big man, in the first half. Thomas had 19 points in the decisive second half and 23 for the game. Indiana took the title with a 63–50 victory.

Thomas was only a sophomore, but that spring he decided not to come back to school. He headed for big money in the NBA.

Thomas had a great career in the NBA. He helped turn the Detroit Pistons, one of the league's weakest teams, into a contender. The Pistons were NBA champions in 1989 and 1990.

After several seasons as a television commentator and general manager of the NBA's Toronto Raptors, Thomas bought the Continental Basketball Association (CBA). He eventually gave up his interest in the CBA to become head coach of the Indiana Pacers.

ISIAH THOMAS

BORN: April 30, 1961, Chicago, Illinois.

HIGH SCHOOL: St. Joseph's High School, Westchester, Illinois.

COLLEGE: Indiana University.

PRO: Detroit Pistons, 1981–1994.

RECORDS: Pistons all-time leader in points (18,882), assists (9,061), and steals (1,861); fourth all-time in NBA assists, 9,061.

HONORS: NCAA Tournament MVP, 1981; All-NBA first team, 1984–1986; NBA All-Star MVP, 1984, 1986; selected as one of the 50 Greatest Players in NBA History, 1996; elected to Naismith Memorial Basketball Hall of Fame, 2000.

Putting the ball on the floor, Isiah Thomas dribbles past his defender.

Internet Address

http://www.nba.com/coachfile/isiah_thomas/index.html?nav=page

JAMES WORTHY

THE 1982 TITLE GAME HAD A GREAT cast of characters. John Thompson was the brilliant six-foot ten-inch coach of the Georgetown Hoyas. He was the first African-American coach to lead a team into the Final.

Thompson's star was Patrick Ewing, a seven-foot giant from Jamaica. His long arms, which stretched eight feet from fingertip to fingertip, terrorized opponents.

Thompson, Ewing, and the Hoyas would be going against Dean Smith and the North Carolina Tar Heels. The Tar Heels lineup featured Sam Perkins, who had suffered through the 1981 loss to Indiana. James Worthy was the star at forward. In a weird coincidence, Worthy would be facing an old high school teammate, Sleepy Floyd of the Hoyas.

In the opening moments, Ewing was a monster. He prowled the court under the Tar Heel basket like a giant moving tree. Over and over he slapped away everything Worthy and his North Carolina teammates shot. Ewing also surprised the Tar Heels with his offensive skills, finishing with 23 points.

Worthy put on an offensive show of his own. He did not take as many shots as Ewing, but he was even more deadly. Out of 17 tries, he made 13. The Tar Heel star finished with 28 points. He also had 3 steals and 4 rebounds.

The game was tight all the way. Late in the second half, Smith told the Tar Heels to stall and take time off the clock. The frustrated Hoyas fouled Matt Doherty with 1:19 left. Two free throws would have given North Carolina a three-point lead. Instead, Doherty missed the first and Ewing got the rebound. Seconds later Floyd released a tough twelve-foot

JAMES WORTHY

In 1982, the North Carolina Tar Heels led by James Worthy, Sam Perkins, and Michael Jordan won the school's first championship in twenty-five years.

jumper. It bounced on the rim and then fell through. Georgetown had a 62–61 lead.

Doherty was heartsick. During a timeout, he looked at Coach Smith and thought, "I had the game in my hands and I lost it for him."[1] Tears filled his eyes.

In the huddle, Smith reminded his players they had thirty-two seconds left to get a shot and win the title. Everybody expected the ball to go to Worthy or Perkins. The coach decided to surprise the Hoyas. The final shot would not be taken by the veterans. Instead, the ball would be in the hands of a freshman—Michael Jordan. As the players returned to the court, Smith whispered, "Knock it in, Michael."[2]

The Tar Heels worked the ball in, and the Hoyas, as expected, concentrated on Worthy and Perkins. Jordan got the ball. He calmly buried a seventeen-footer, and North Carolina led, 63–62.

Georgetown still had time. Fred Brown dribbled across half court, then stopped and looked for teammate Eric Smith. As Smith suddenly took off for the hoop, Worthy stepped between the two Hoyas. Then, in one of the most disastrous passes of all time, Brown flipped the ball directly to Worthy.

"If I had a rubber band," Brown said later, "I'd have brought it back."[3] But, of course, he did not, and the game was over.

For his points and his crucial steal, Worthy would be named the tournament's Most Outstanding Player. He then moved on to a fine pro career with the Los Angeles Lakers. Playing alongside Kareem Abdul-Jabbar and Magic Johnson, he helped bring the Lakers NBA championships in 1985, 1987, and 1988.

JAMES WORTHY

BORN: February 27, 1961, Gastonia, North Carolina.

HIGH SCHOOL: Ashbrook High School, Gastonia, North Carolina.

COLLEGE: University of North Carolina.

PRO: Los Angeles Lakers, 1982–1994.

HONORS: NCAA Tournament MVP, 1982; NBA Finals MVP, 1988; selected as one of the 50 Greatest Players in NBA History, 1996.

James Worthy bears down defensively in a game against Maryland in January 1981.

Internet Address

http://www.jamesworthy.com

GLEN RICE

Flying above the rim, Michigan's Glen Rice throws down an easy basket.

GLEN RICE

WHEN THE 1988–89 REGULAR SEASON WAS OVER, the Michigan Wolverines were in trouble. Their coach, Bill Frieder, had signed a contract with Arizona State for the next season. The university promptly dismissed him. Steve Fisher, a Michigan assistant, was hired as interim coach.

Then the Wolverines had to face the postseason NCAA tournament under the leadership of an inexperienced, untested coach. Hardly anybody expected them to be around for long. But Xavier of Ohio and Southern Alabama fell to the Wolverines in the early rounds. After Fisher's men clipped the Tar Heels of North Carolina, 92–87, fans began to take notice.

After clobbering Virginia, 102–65, Michigan found itself in the Final Four. Illinois, the No. 1 seed in the Midwest, was heavily favored. Earlier in the season, the Wolverines had lost twice to the Fighting Illini. The Final Four match was different. With forward Glen Rice leading the effort, Michigan won, 83–81.

In the Final, Rice and the Wolverines faced another surprise team, the Seton Hall Pirates, who had begun the tournament as the West Regional's No. 3 seed. Early on, the game looked like a walk. Michigan had a 51–39 advantage with 14:30 to go. Then Seton Hall's John Morton took over.

Morton scored twenty-five of his thirty-five points in the second half, seventeen of them in just eight minutes. With 2:13 to go, the Pirates finally led, 67–66.

Daryll Walker sank a Seton Hall free throw just before Rice rose to the occasion. After the Wolverines grabbed a rebound, he raced downcourt. A long shot was good for three! Michigan was ahead, 69–68.

Sean Higgins got two free throws to make it 71–68. Morton tied the game with a three-pointer. The Wolverines worked the clock down, then got the ball to Rice for a final shot. It missed, forcing overtime.

The Pirates jumped out, 79–76, with 1:35 remaining in OT. Morton had a chance to put the game on ice, but his shot missed. Terry Mills of Michigan wound up with the ball. He made a move, then released a tricky turnaround jumper. Good! Seton Hall's lead was down to 79–78.

The Pirates whittled down the clock to just eleven seconds. Then Morton took another potential title-clinching shot. He missed again. Michigan's Rumeal Robinson grabbed the rebound and took off.

Robinson was fouled. His first shot was good! Tie game! Robinson kept cool, and the second shot was as good as the first. Michigan 80, Seton Hall 79!

Desperately, the Pirates ran down the length of the court. Just before the buzzer, Walker heaved a shot. It slammed off the backboard—right into the hands of Rice.

Seconds later Robinson jumped into his teammate's arms. "We're No. 1! We're No. 1!" they screamed together.[1] Michigan had its first NCAA championship. Steve Fisher, the interim coach, was 6–0. "I'm the happiest man alive," he shouted. "All our kids did a great job."[2]

Robinson and Higgins had made the clutch, game-winning shots, but it was Rice who had supplied most of the points. In the Final, he had scored 31. He also got 11 rebounds.

Rice had one of the greatest six-game tournaments ever. His 1989 performance set records for most points (184), most field goals (75), and most three-pointers (27).

GLEN RICE

BORN: May 28, 1967, Jacksonville, Arkansas.

HIGH SCHOOL: Northwestern Community High School, Flint, Michigan.

COLLEGE: University of Michigan.

PRO: Miami Heat, 1989–1995; Charlotte Hornets, 1995–1998; Los Angeles Lakers, 1998–2000.

RECORDS: Set NCAA Tournament record for most points in one tournament, (184).

HONORS: NCAA Tournament MVP, 1989; NBA All-Star MVP, 1997.

After his stellar career at the University of Michigan, Glen Rice was drafted by the Miami Heat.

Internet Address
http://www.nba.com/playerfile/glen_rice/index.html?nav=page

CHRISTIAN LAETTNER

AS THE DUKE BLUE DEVILS WERE BEING WHIPPED by North Carolina, Christian Laettner swore at his teammates. After the game Coach Mike Krzyzewski got in the star's face: "The yelling, this whole thing. You were bad, Christian, and that bothers me because you're not bad . . . but if you do that in the tournament, you're not going to play."[1]

Laettner got the message, and he worked hard to keep his temper under control. He wanted to live up to Duke University's classy image. The Blue Devils had a steady, patient offense and a tight defense. No hotdogging. Just good solid basketball.

When Duke met UNLV in the 1990 NCAA Final, the Runnin' Rebels destroyed the Blue Devils, 103–73. In 1991, Coach K, Laettner, and the rest of the Blue Devils would not be satisfied with just a regional title. They wanted a national championship, but to get into the Final, they would have to face the Runnin' Rebels again.

Unlike the 1990 title match, this game was close all the way. This time it came down to Laettner at the free-throw line. With 12.7 seconds left, the score was tied, 77–77. During the time-out before the shots, Krzyzewski smiled and asked, "You all right?"[2]

Laettner grinned back and nodded. Then he sank both shots and the Runnin' Rebels were gone.

The Final was almost anticlimactic. Laettner's 18 points and 10 rebounds helped the Blue Devils beat Kansas, 72–65. He was named Most Outstanding Player of the tournament.

Once again during the 1991–92 season, Duke was one of the nation's toughest teams. In the regional final, Coach K's

Christian Laettner shoots the game-winning shot against Kentucky in the NCAA East Finals in 1992.

CHRISTIAN LAETTNER

team met Kentucky in one of the sport's most memorable games. In the first half, Laettner rewrote the record books by passing Houston's Elvin Hayes as the all-time scoring leader in tournament history.

After regulation play ended in a tie, the battle continued into overtime. With 2.1 seconds left in OT, Kentucky led, 103–102. After a timeout, Grant Hill inbounded the ball by tossing it almost the length of the court to Laettner.

Laettner dribbled once, faked both ways, then went up with a high, arcing shot. Nothing but net! The buzzer sounded. Duke won, 104–103.

In one of the most important games of his college career, under incredible pressure, the Duke star had what many would call "The Perfect Game." He took 10 shots from the floor and 10 free throws—without missing a single shot!

Duke beat Indiana, 81–78 in the semifinal game. Now, the Final was billed as a battle of opposites. Duke, the steady, disciplined team, was matched against the exciting, trash-talking, hotdogging Wolverines from Michigan. Coach Steve Fisher had recruited five of the best high school players in the nation—and all of them were starting as freshmen. Reporters called them the Fab Five.

After a close first half, the Blue Devils blew the Wolverines away, 71–51.

Laettner's college career was finally over. He and the Blue Devils had battled their way into three NCAA Finals. They had won a pair of national championships, and nobody had ever scored more tournament points than Laettner.

CHRISTIAN LAETTNER

BORN: August 17, 1969, Angola, New York.

HIGH SCHOOL: Nichols School, Buffalo, New York.

COLLEGE: Duke University.

PRO: Minnesota Timberwolves, 1992–1996; Atlanta Hawks, 1996–1998; Detroit Pistons, 1998–2000.

RECORDS: Set NCAA record for most career points in NCAA tournament play (407); set NCAA record for most games played at the Division I level, (148).

HONORS: NCAA Tournament MVP, 1991; College Player of the Year, 1992; Olympic gold medalist, 1992.

Laettner celebrates after hitting a game-winning shot against Connecticut in the NCAA Tournament in 1990.

Internet Address

http://www.nba.com/playerfile/christian_laettner/index.html?nav=page

MILES SIMON

Arizona's Miles Simon dribbles the ball during the second half of the NCAA championship game on March 31, 1997.

THERE HAD BEEN A LOT OF TOUGH BATTLES before the Arizona Wildcats and Miles Simon got to the 1997 NCAA Championship Game. In the third round of the postseason, they faced No. 1-ranked Kansas. Arizona's tenacious defense rattled the Jayhawks, forcing twenty turnovers. The Wildcats won, 85–82.

Up by three in a thriller against Providence, Simon's three-point shot was blocked. Jamel Thomas's three-pointer then tied the game, sending it into overtime. After Simon's jumper at 2:53, they never trailed. Providence fell, 96–92.

The North Carolina Tar Heels, No. 1 in the East Regional, were next. At first, it looked like a blowout. North Carolina romped to a 15–4 advantage. Then the Wildcats composed themselves and began whittling the margin. Just before the half, a bucket and a free throw from Simon put Arizona ahead, 34–31.

In the second half, teammate Mike Bibby buried four straight three-pointers, and it was all over. The Wildcats won, 66–58. Next was the war with Kentucky, No. 1 seed in the West and the defending champion.

In the first half, the referees thought the Kentucky defenders were playing too tight. Over and over the whistles blew. Simon took 11 free throws and made 9. He also dropped in 3 shots from the floor. At intermission, his team led, 33–32.

Bibby's 14 points kept Arizona ahead through most of the second half. Simon added 11 more of his own. He drove Rick Pitino's men crazy by repeatedly dribbling past the Kentucky defenders and working his way toward the hoop for a shot or a pass. "He has fakes," Pitino said. "He's a wonderful, wonderful player."[1]

The Kentucky fouls kept coming, forcing several of their starters to the bench. That meant Ron Mercer, Kentucky's leading scorer, could not rest himself. The Kentucky press was not getting the job done. "We were able to break it and break it," Simon said. "Eventually, running ninety-four feet the whole game, they got tired."[2]

Of course, the Kentucky players were not the only ones getting tired. "They wore me down," Simon said. "I was very tired. I called for subs three times."[3]

The score was 74–71 with twenty seconds left. Kentucky's Anthony Epps took off downcourt and tossed in a three to tie the game and force overtime.

Early on in OT, Mercer had a chance to tap in a rebound and give Kentucky the lead, but he and his team seemed to be out of gas. For three minutes, Mercer and his teammates were shut out. They missed 6 of their last 7 shots.

Meanwhile they kept picking up the fouls and Arizona kept heading for the free-throw line. By then, Simon was dragging, too. "I had to suck it up."[4] When the pressure was on, Simon came through, hitting 4 straight charity shots in the last forty-one seconds. "When I was shooting my last free throws," he said, "I had chills running through my body."[5]

When the overtime ended, Arizona had hit on 34 free-throw attempts, compared to only 9 for Kentucky. Simon scored 30 points.

Arizona won, 84–79, to claim its first national championship. After Simon got his MOP trophy, he said, "This is the most unbelievable thing I've ever done."[6]

MILES SIMON

BORN: November 21, 1975, Stockholm, Sweden.

HIGH SCHOOL: Mater Dei, Santa Ana, California.

COLLEGE: University of Arizona.

PRO: Orlando Magic, 1998.

HONORS: NCAA Final Four Most Outstanding Player, 1997; First
Team All-American, 1998.

Simon clutches the ball after helping lead Arizona past Kentucky in
the 1997 national championship game.

Internet Address

http://wildcat.arizona.edu/papers/90/124/01_1_m.html

RICHARD HAMILTON

The University of Connecticut's Richard Hamilton goes up for a dunk during a game from November 1998.

RICHARD HAMILTON

BIG MONEY FROM THE PROS ALMOST LURED Richard Hamilton away from the University of Connecticut in the spring of 1998. He had just earned the Big East Player of the Year award, and the Huskies had already won a pair of league titles.

"We won the Big East but never the national championship," Hamilton remembered. "I thought about that. I didn't want to end my season on a loss. The only thing I could do about it was come back and play."[1]

Almost as soon as he decided to stick with the Huskies, Hamilton found himself out of action. During tryouts for the summer World Championships, he broke his foot. He was stuck at home while the foot healed. Much of the time he spent with his biggest fan—his grandfather, Edward Hamilton. Ever since Richard had been a freshman in high school, the older man had cut out clippings of articles about his grandson. They were taped to the wall around his television. The summer of 1998 would be the last time the two of them could be together. Richard's grandfather was dying from lung cancer.

"It killed me not to play," the Huskie star said, "but I got to see my grandfather just about every day until he died. I'm told things happen for a reason. Maybe they do."[2]

Hamilton remembered his grandfather by having a new tattoo on his arm. It was a cross with the words "EDWARD HAMILTON, OCT. 9, 1922–SEPT. 25, 1998." After the funeral, he sadly asked his father, "Who's going to put up those new clippings next to the television set?"[3]

Hamilton's foot healed, and he helped Connecticut to a

fine 1998–99 season. The Huskies did so well, in fact, that they made it to the 1999 NCAA Final. Unfortunately for them, their opponents would be the No. 1-rated team in the nation, the mighty Duke Blue Devils.

Coach Jim Calhoun and the Huskies had no intention of fading in the Final. The coach told his men they had to keep moving on offense. Somehow, they had to shut down Elton Brand, Duke's superstar. Calhoun called his strategy "big-to-big double team."[4] Every time Brand got the ball, he was going to be smothered by a pair of Huskies.

Hamilton's father was not worried about the point spread. Just before the game he told his son, "Grandpa wants a national championship."[5]

Calhoun's game plan worked. Brand had a frustrating evening. "They made it really tough to get open looks," he said. "They were fighting every possession, every time I touched it."[6]

Meanwhile Connecticut's offense was matching Duke's point for point. With a 68–68 tie and just 3:50 left, Hamilton was rammed by Duke's Chris Carrawell. He doubled over and gasped. Was he hurt? No, just catching his breath.

After he straightened up, Hamilton made two free throws. Then Ricky Moore stole the ball and flipped it to him. The three-pointer was good! UConn led, 73–68.

At just under ten seconds the lead was 77–74. Duke's Trajan Langdon had the ball. A three-pointer would tie it up. But he was called for travelling to end the game. Connecticut had won the national title!

The game was especially sweet for Hamilton, of course. There would be more newspaper clippings than ever. At crunch time, he had come through, picking up 27 points.

"You can't describe it," he said. "I still don't understand what we accomplished."[7] In the arm with the tattoo, he held the trophy for Most Outstanding Player.

RICHARD HAMILTON

BORN: February 14, 1978, Coatesville, Pennsylvania.

HIGH SCHOOL: Coatesville High School.

COLLEGE: University of Connecticut.

PRO: Washington Wizards, 1999– .

HONORS: Second Team All-American, 1998; First Team All-American, 1999; NCAA Final Four Most Outstanding Player, 1999.

Richard Hamilton helped lead UConn to its first national title in 1999.

Internet Address

http://www.nba.com/playerfile/richard_hamilton/index.html?nav=page

Chapter Notes

Bill Bradley

1. Billy Packer with Roland Lazenby, *50 Years of the Final Four* (Dallas: Taylor Publishing, 1987), p. 9.

Kareem Abdul-Jabbar

1. Kareem Abdul-Jabbar with Mignon McCarthy, *Kareem* (New York: Random House, 1990), p. 11.

Bill Walton

1. Bill Walton with Gene Wojchiechowski, *Nothing but Net: Just Give Me the Ball and Get Out of the Way* (New York: Hyperion, 1994), p. 1.

2. Billy Packer with Roland Lazenby, *50 Years of the Final Four* (Dallas: Taylor Publishing, 1987), p. 114.

3. Ibid.

Magic Johnson

1. Gary Stein, Gannett News Service dispatch from Salt Lake City, March 27, 1979.

2. Ibid.

3. Associated Press dispatch from Salt Lake City, March 27, 1979.

4. Stein.

Isiah Thomas

1. Mike Lopresti, Gannett News Service dispatch from Philadelphia, March 31, 1981.

2. Ibid.

James Worthy

1. Malcolm Moran, "North Carolina Slips Past Georgetown by 63–62," *The New York Times*, March 30, 1982, p. C9.

2. Alan Minsky, *March to the Finals* (New York: MetroBooks, 1999), p. 78.

3. "Stolen Pass Haunts Brown," *The New York Times*, March 30, 1982, p. D11.

Glen Rice

1. Thomas George, "'We're No. 1' Has a Nice Ring to It," *The New York Times*, April 4, 1989, p. A24.

2. William C. Rhoden, "Michigan Works Overtime, but It's Worth It," *The New York Times*, April 4, 1989, p. A19.

Christian Laettner

1. Greg Doyel, *Coach K: Building the Duke Dynasty* (Lenexa, Kans.: Addax Publishing Group, Inc., 1999), p. 138.

2. Ibid., p. 148.

Miles Simon

1. Alan Minsky, *March to the Finals* (New York: MetroBooks, 1999), p. 110.

2. Hal Bock, Associated Press dispatch from Indianapolis, April 1, 1997.

3. Ibid.

4. Ibid.

5. Mike Lopresti, Gannett News Service dispatch from Indianapolis, April 1, 1997.

6. Minsky, p. 111.

Richard Hamilton

1. Associated Press dispatch from St. Petersburg, Fla., March 30, 1999.

2. Jack McCallum, "Conn Artists," *Sports Illustrated*, April 5, 1999, <http://www.britannica.com/bcom/magazine/article/0,5744,84954,00.html> (July 31, 2000).

3. Jim Calhoun with Leigh Montville, *Dare to Dream* (New York: Broadway Books, 1999), p. 107.

4. McCallum.

5. Ibid.

6. Mike DeCourcy, "Connecticut 77, Duke 74: Turnovers Squash Blue Devils' Quest for Classic Ending," *Cincinnati Enquirer*, March 30, 1999, <http://enquirer.com/editions/1999/03/30/spt_connecticut_77_duke.html.>

7. Associated Press dispatch from St. Petersburg, Fla., March 29, 1999.

INDEX

A

Abdul-Jabbar, Kareem (Lew Alcindor), 10–13, 20, 28

B

Bibby, Mike, 39
Bird, Larry, 16, 18, 20
Black, Jimmy, 22
Bradley, Bill, 6–9
Brand, Elton, 44
Brown, Fred, 28
Bush, George W., 8

C

Calhoun, Jim, 44
Carrawell, Chris, 44
Charles, Ron, 20

D

Doherty, Matt, 26, 28
Donnelly, Terry, 18, 20

E

Epps, Anthony, 40
Ewing, Patrick, 26, 28

F

Fisher, Steve, 31, 32, 36
Floyd, Sleepy, 26, 28
Frieder, Bill, 31

G

Gore, Al, 8
Graziano, Rocky, 15

H

Hamilton, Edward, 43, 44
Hamilton, Richard, 42–45
Hayes, Elvin, 11–12, 36
Heathcote, 18, 20
Higgins, Sean, 32
Hill, Grant, 36

J

Johnson, Earvin Magic, 18–21, 28
Jordan, Michael, 28

K

Kelser, Greg, 20
Knight, Bobby, 22, 24
Krzyzewski, Mike, 34, 36

L

Laettner, Christian, 34–37
Langdon, Trajan, 44

M

Mercer, Ron, 40
Mills, Terry, 32
Moore, Ricky, 44
Morton, John, 31, 32

N

National Collegiate Athletic Association (NCAA), 4
National Invitational Tournament (NIT), 4

P

Perkins, Sam, 24, 26
Pitino, Rick, 39–40

R

Rice, Glen, 30–33
Robinson, Rumeal, 32
Russell, Cazzie, 8

S

Simon, Miles, 38–41
Smith, Dean, 24, 26, 28
Smith, Eric, 28

T

Thomas, Isiah, 22–25
Thomas, Jamel, 39
Thompson, John, 26
Turner, Landon, 24

V

van Breda Kolff, Butch, 8

W

Walker, Daryll, 31, 32
Walton, Bill, 14–17
Wittman, Randy, 22
Wooden, John, 11, 15
Worthy, James, 26–29